Ready to Fly

How Sylvia Townsend Became the Bookmobile Ballerina

Story told by **Lea Lyon** and **A. LaFaye**   Foreword by **Sylvia Townsend**

Illustrated by **Jessica Gibson**

HARPER

An Imprint of HarperCollinsPublishers

For Sylvia, who was kind enough to share her story with me,
and for my dear friend Mary Ann, who introduced me to
the amazing bookmobile ballerina.
—L.L.

For Regan: Know your own worth,
celebrate your gifts, spread your wings, and fly!
—A.L.

To my loving, supportive family,
especially my mother, who always believed in my creative talent.
—J.G.

Ready to Fly: How Sylvia Townsend Became the Bookmobile Ballerina · Text copyright © 2020 by Lea Lyon and Alexandria LaFaye · Illustrations copyright © 2020 by Jessica Gibson · All rights reserved. Printed in the United States of America. · No part of this book may be used or reproduced in any manner whatsoever without written permission except in the case of brief quotations embodied in critical articles and reviews. For information address HarperCollins Children's Books, a division of HarperCollins Publishers, 195 Broadway, New York, NY 10007. · www.harpercollinschildrens.com · Library of Congress Control Number: 2018961752 · ISBN 978-0-06-288878-5 The artist used Photoshop CC and a Wacom Cintiq drawing tablet to create the digital illustrations for this book. · Typography by Honee Jang 20 21 22 23 PC 10 9 8 7 6 5 4 3 2 ❖ First Edition

A Note on Hopes and Dreams

I believe every child is born with gifts.

As a child, my gifts were reading, dancing, and singing, which all helped me teach myself the basics of ballet from the instruction books I found in the bookmobile.

Even with these gifts, I grew up very poor and didn't have a lot of money or resources available to me. Luckily, my parents, who were rich in other ways, would give me words of encouragement and shower me with their support. My father went as far as surprising me with a pair of ballet shoes from the secondhand store. My parents helped me pursue my dreams of becoming a ballerina and opening my own school of dance.

I hope every parent will pay close attention to their children. I hope parents will be ready to help children become the best versions of themselves, whether they want to sing, dance, or act or become an athlete, scientist, or doctor.

I hope this book will inspire children everywhere to pursue their dreams regardless of race or background, whether they are rich or poor. I want every child to forget the phrase *I cannot* and to always know that

yes, you can!

—Sylvia Robertson Townsend

Born with the beat in my feet, I jive to Daddy's jazz
and sway to Mama's symphonies.

As musical notes start to float, I rise to my toes,
ready to fly.

When our secondhand TV fills with beautiful dancers,
all feathered and fine, I say, "I want to do that too!"
"Sylvia," Mama says, "they're dancing the ballet *Swan Lake*."
"Ballet? Oh, I need to learn ballet!" Sylvia says. "Can I take lessons?"

"I want to **leap**

and **twirl**

and do **pliés**
till I can dance in real ballets."

But Daddy says, "Sorry, baby, lessons don't come free."

So I twist Mama's scarves into a tutu
and make my *own* ballet slippers.
Dressed and ready, I try and try, but
my feet won't budge.

There must be another way to learn how to soar.

That spring, a bookmobile rolls into our neighborhood.

"Do you have any ballet books?"
I ask the smiling librarian.
"Why don't we look together?"
We search the shelves for the perfect
book to give me wings.

At home, I begin reading, building my own barre,
learning the positions—first, second, and third.

Each month, a new book adds to my routine.
Jeté, pirouette, arabesque.
I feel my wings growing one feather at a time.

One day, I'll be a flying ballerina too.

News of the "bookmobile ballerina" draws
neighborhood kids, singing,
"Teach *us* how to
Leap and **twirl** and do **pliés**
till *we* can dance in real ballets."

Out on the stoop, I show them my swan-like strides and my rising relevés.
I'm the one giving the lessons now!

My fourth-grade teacher, Miss Speidel, sees
my swirling steps.
"Any girl who can dance like you needs real
lessons to reach for the sky," she says, and offers
to pay my way.

Mama, Miss Speidel, and I set off to see some
ballet schools.

But the first school says, "Too full."

School two says, "No room."

School three whispers, "It just can't be," letting
the real reason slip—ballet is for white girls.

Is ballet *not* for girls like me?

Those words pluck the
feathers from my wings.

My dancing feet
don't feel the beat.

My tutu goes back to
being Mama's scarves.

I tuck away my slippers and tell the librarian I won't need more books.

But my little swans twirl up for their next lesson.
They still want to fly.
Who else will show them how if I don't?

Lesson by lesson,

we grow more feathers, until . . .

. . . we sashay onto the school talent show stage in the fall.

As the last notes fade away, I float into **reverence.**
I hold my breath, waiting to hear what Mme. Sawicka will say.

Smiling, she says, "You've never had a lesson, dear?"
I bow my head, whispering, "No."
"Well, you're a beautiful dancer."

Mme. Sawicka takes me under her wing, offering me a free place in her school.

Every book, every beat, every practice at the
barre has brought me to this day.

All feathered and fine,
I am a ballerina who can
leap and twirl and do pliés
and loves to dance in real ballets.

A ballerina whose little swans are ready to fly.

Sylvia Robertson Townsend, born 1943

I heard the story of the bookmobile ballerina from Sylvia Townsend herself at her dance studio in Richmond, California, where she's been teaching ballet to children of all backgrounds, from around the San Francisco Bay Area, for over forty years.

Sylvia grew up in a small apartment with eight siblings, two parents, and lots of music. Here, she created her "own little corner of the world," scouring the TV for dance shows. "I had 'Bette Davis eyes' and would practice my 'Bette Davis walk' and scat like Ella [Fitzgerald]!" she told me, and, pointing to herself, said, "This 'skinny little black kid' was into every form of dance."

But Sylvia lived in a segregated 1950s America. People then lived by "unofficial rules" and laws that made certain things "for white people only." African Americans weren't allowed in specific restaurants, hotels, or pools. In the South, they were forced to use separate drinking fountains, schools, and seating sections on the bus. Though there were a few black professional ballerinas, such as Janet Collins and Raven Wilkinson, Sylvia soon learned that ballet was usually "for white girls only."

Her father was her first hero and biggest fan. "He would talk to me about Buffalo Soldiers and the Tuskegee Airmen" who fought discrimination and won, Sylvia recounted. "He told me, 'See these big buildings? You don't have to work in them; you can own one.'"

Sylvia remembers the first time she stepped into the bookmobile. The librarian gave her a little sitting stool, and she "would go through all the library books and find her ballet books." She read books about ballet positions and steps and famous ballets with their glorious costumes. "I was the happiest child on earth," she told me.

As a teenager, Sylvia met Alexandra Sawicka (pronounced *Shaviska*), who became her second-biggest fan, ballet instructor, and mentor. They remained friends for many years, having daily tea parties over the phone.

Sylvia was a spunky, courageous girl. And with hard work, a supportive family, devoted teachers, and library books, she did become a ballerina. Sylvia created her own dance company, which performed nationwide, and her own ballet school called the Art of Ballet School of Dance.

Some of Sylvia's students performed at Disneyland and later trained with famous dancers such as Alvin Ailey and Debbie Allen. Her son danced with the Dance Theatre of Harlem, and her two daughters taught at and codirected Sylvia's school.

Much has changed since Sylvia was a child. In 1990, Lauren Anderson became the first African American principal ballerina at the historically white Houston Ballet company. Today, African American Misty Copeland is a principal dancer at the famous American Ballet Theatre. And now, ballet lessons are mostly available to children of all colors who can afford them. Slowly, equality is growing in our country, but we have a long way to go.

Sylvia did reach her dream of becoming a ballerina. And it all started with one determined girl with one library book from one bookmobile.

A Brief History of the Bookmobile

A bookmobile is a traveling library—a van or truck that goes to various towns or schools, bringing library books to many people, complete with a librarian to help them find the perfect one. Many small marginalized communities didn't have a library. Bookmobiles changed that reality.

Bookmobiles in the United States

The very first book wagon in the U.S. (Maryland, 1905)

In the early 1900s, traveling libraries first became popular in the United States. Horse-drawn carts, then, later, cars and trucks, were used to deliver boxes of books to remote library stations, leaving books in the post office or another special place to act as a library.

Ms. Mary Titcomb designed the first bookmobile in the United States in 1905. Equipped with shelves for two hundred books, she would open the doors of the bookmobile and check books out to people. Inside the horse-drawn wagon there was a space for cartons of books that Mary would leave at the book-deposit stations.

Over time, bookmobiles were motorized and became the libraries themselves. They would drive into a town and open their doors, and children and adults would get to check out books to borrow until the next visit. Then on to another town.

Today's Bookmobiles

After experiencing a decline in the 1970s and '80s, bookmobiles have made a twenty-first-century comeback. Today's colorful bookmobiles get kids excited even before they see the books they can borrow.

With the addition of available computers, public libraries have become more popular. New digital bookmobiles, full of equipment like computers and printers, as well as books, still delight and inspire thousands of children like Sylvia Townsend every year.

Busy young readers in the Liberty, TX, school district bookmobile.

Bookmobiles through the Decades

| 1920s | Bookmobile of the Saint Paul Public Library (Minnesota, 1917) |

| 1930s | WDA Circulating Book Truck (Union County, SC, 1937) |

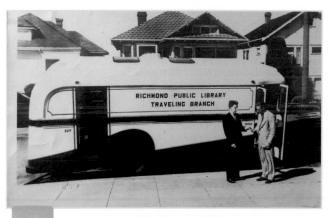

| 1940s | The Richmond Public Library Traveling Branch (California, 1948) |

Fun fact: In 1947, Richmond, California, Sylvia's hometown, was the first city on the West Coast to have a bookmobile.

| 1950s | Children lining up at the Rockingham County Library bookmobile (North Carolina, 1955) |

| 1960s | Bookmobile of Leon County (Florida, 1965) |

| Today | City of Richmond's bookmobile (California, 2018) |

Photo Credits

References

- "Another History of Bookmobiles," http://eduscapes.com/history/contemporary/1930.htm.
- "Blacks and Classical Dance," December 2008, https://ferris.edu/HTMLS/news/jimcrow/question/2008/december.htm.
- "A Brief History of Bookmobiles," Chronicle Books Blog, April 11, 2018, https://www.chroniclebooks.com/blog/2018/04/11/brief-history-bookmobiles-america/
- Gia Kourlas, "Where Are All the Black Swans?" *New York Times*, May 6, 2007.
- Margaret Fuhrer, "Raven Wilkinson's Extraordinary Life: An Exclusive Interview," https://www.pointemagazine.com/raven-wilkinson-interview-2412812564.html.
- Spencer Whitney, "Art of Ballet School Thrives in Richmond," *Richmond Confidential*, July 25, 2012.
- Thalia Mara and Lee Wyndham, *First Steps in Ballet* (Garden City, NY: Doubleday & Co., 1955).

For Further Reading

- *Ballerina Dreams: From Orphan to Dancer*, by Michaela DePrince and Elaine DePrince and illustrated by Frank Morrison (Random House, 2014)
- *Beautiful Ballerina*, by Marilyn Nelson and illustrated by Susan Kuklin (Scholastic, 2009)
- *Black Dance in America: A History Through Its People*, by James Haskins (HarperCollins, 1992)
- *Dancing in the Wings*, by Debbie Allen and illustrated by Kadir Nelson (Puffin Books, 2003)
- *Firebird*, by Misty Copeland and illustrated by Christopher Myers (G.P. Putnam's Sons, 2014)
- *A Girl Named Misty: The True Story of Misty Copeland* (American Girl), by Kelly Starling Lyons and illustrated by Melissa Manwill (Scholastic, 2018)
- *Library on Wheels: Mary Lemist Titcomb and America's First Bookmobile*, by Sharlee Glenn (Abrams, 2018)
- *Life in Motion: An Unlikely Ballerina Young Readers Edition*, by Misty Copeland (Aladdin, 2016)
- *Trailblazer: The Story of Ballerina Raven Wilkinson*, by Leda Schubert and illustrated by Theodore Taylor III (Little Bee Books, 2018)